AUNT NINA AND HER NEPHEWS AND NIECES

by Franz Brandenberg   illustrated by Aliki

 GREENWILLOW BOOKS
New York

For Tante Nindli

Library of Congress Cataloging in Publication Data

Brandenberg, Franz.
Aunt Nina and her nephews and nieces.
Summary: When Aunt Nina gives a birthday party
for her cat, the guests receive surprise presents.
[1. Parties—Fiction. 2. Birthdays—Fiction.
3. Cats—Fiction] I. Aliki, ill. II. Title.
PZ7.B7364Au 1983   [E]   82-12004
ISBN 0-688-01869-6
ISBN 0-688-01870-X (lib. bdg.)

AUNT NINA AND HER NEPHEWS AND NIECES

Aunt Nina had no children.
She had no husband, either.
But she had three nephews
and three nieces.

The nephews and nieces liked
to visit Aunt Nina.

One year, on her cat's birthday,
Aunt Nina invited all six of them.

"Shall we go to the zoo, the toy shop,
the theater, the haunted house, or
a restaurant? Or would you like to have
a treasure hunt?" asked Aunt Nina.

"Couldn't we just stay home?"
said the nephews and nieces.
"If you like," said Aunt Nina.

"Where is Fluffy, the birthday cat?"
  asked the children.
"She must be hiding," said Aunt Nina.
"Let's look for her!" said the children.

They started in the basement.
They found rabbits, turtles,
guinea pigs, and mice.
But no Fluffy.
"This is better than the zoo,"
they said.

They went to the first floor.
They found dolls, teddy bears,
jumping jacks,
music boxes, jigsaw puzzles,
trains, tin soldiers, and books.
But no Fluffy.
"This is better than the toy shop,"
they said.

They went to the second floor.
They found dresses, shoes,
jewelry, makeup, and wigs.
But no Fluffy.
"This is better than the theater,"
they said.

They went to the attic.
They found blowing curtains, flying
bats, old suitcases, a lot of dust.
But no Fluffy.
"This is better than the haunted
house," they said.

"Don't worry about Fluffy," said Aunt
Nina. "She'll show up for her party."
"I wish I had a cat of my own," said
one of the nephews.
"So do I! And I! And I! And I!
And I!" said all the others.

"Who is hungry?" asked Aunt Nina.
"We are!" said all the children.
"All right, let's have lunch," said Aunt Nina.
 They went to the kitchen and had lunch.
"This is better than a restaurant," they said.

"Nap time!" said Aunt Nina.
"We don't take naps," said the children.
"Today you do," said Aunt Nina.
"So you will be rested for the party."
She walked them up to her bed,
pulled back the covers....

"There is Fluffy!" said the children.
"And what's that?"
 Under Fluffy were six newborn kittens.
"What a birthday!" said Aunt Nina.
"This is better than a treasure hunt,"
 said the children.
"Now let's leave them alone," said Aunt
 Nina. "They don't like to be disturbed."
"That takes care of our naps," said
 the nephews and nieces.

The children unpacked Fluffy's birthday presents. Aunt Nina brought in Fluffy's birthday cake. They all sang,

"Happy birthday to you,
happy birthday to you,
happy birthday, dear Fluffy,
(and all the little Fluffies),
happy birthday to you."

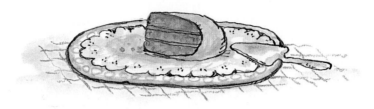

It was time to go home.

"Come see us soon, Aunt Nina!" said
the nephews and nieces.

"I will have to," said Aunt Nina.
"To bring you the kittens when they
are a little bigger. There is one for
each of you."

"This was better than our own
birthdays," said the nephews
and nieces.